BANANA SPLITS

It was like an operating room scene. Intense and quiet. It was time for the bananas.

Goober glanced over at me. "Got a bowl?" he whispered.

I nodded and got one out.

"We'll want to wash the bananas," he said.

Goober carefully placed each banana in the bowl of water before he peeled it, glancing over at me each time. "Now you're sure you won't mind if I cut into them?" he asked, his eyes bulging. "That's a lot of bananas to kill."

"Tell you what," I whispered. "You cut them. I just won't watch, okay?"

BANANA TWIST

"Told with sparkling ease, this wacky story oozes funny situations at every turn of the page."

—*Booklist*

"Brisk, cute and given a boost by the total twist of an ending."

—*Kirkus Reviews*

Banana Twist

Florence Parry Heide

A BANTAM SKYLARK BOOK®
TORONTO · NEW YORK · LONDON · SYDNEY · AUCKLAND

With much love to Don, my husband

*This low-priced Bantam Book
has been completely reset in a type face
designed for easy reading, and was printed
from new plates. It contains the complete
text of the original hard-cover edition.*
NOT ONE WORD HAS BEEN OMITTED.

RL 5, 008-012

BANANA TWIST

*A Bantam Book / published by arrangement with
Holiday House, Inc.*

PRINTING HISTORY

*Holiday House edition published September 1978
4 printings through July 1981
Bantam Skylark edition / November 1982*

*Skylark Books is a registered trademark of Bantam Books, Inc.,
Registered in U.S. Patent and Trademark Office and elsewhere.*

ISBN 0-553-15159-2

Published simultaneously in the United States and Canada

---

*Bantam Books are published by Bantam Books, Inc. Its trade-
mark, consisting of the words "Bantam Books" and the por-
trayal of a rooster, is Registered in U.S. Patent and Trademark
Office and in other countries. Marca Registrada. Bantam
Books, Inc., 666 Fifth Avenue, New York, New York 10103.*

PRINTED IN THE UNITED STATES OF AMERICA

0 9 8

Contents

1 • Something We Don't Tell Parents, 7
2 • You Make Your Friends,
     I'll Make Mine, 19
3 • Who's Got Problems?, 33
4 • The Banana Boy, 47
5 • It Has a Lot to Do with the Stars, 59
6 • A Stroke of Genius, 67
7 • It Was Hopeless, So I Didn't
     Try Too Hard, 83
8 • This Calls for a Celebration, 95
9 • Only the Beginning, 105

1·Something We Don't Tell Parents

I'd been studying the Fairlee Questionnaire so long my brain had callouses. If I really wanted to get into their school, I had to figure out what they really wanted to hear.

These questions were something. If they'd had true or false or multiple choice, I'd have managed. For instance:

CHECK ONE. YOUR NAME IS:
   Queen Victoria
   Alexander the Great
   Jonah D. Krock

or TRUE OR FALSE? GEORGE WASHINGTON IN-
VENTED TELEVISION.

or CIRCLE ONE. YOUR AGE IS:
    Between 0–10
    Between 10–20
    Between 20–30
    Between 30–40

And so on.

But this particular question that I was anguish-
ing over was: Will you tell us something about
yourself?

The page had been blank a long time, as blank
as I was, but I finally pulled myself together, as
together as I ever am. It took a lot of time to
come up with what I came up with, time I could
have spent concentrating on TV.

*Jonah D. Krock is my name. It's a name that
will last me all my life. You can't say that for
everything you've got.*

  *Jonah D. Krock was who I was when I was
a little baby, and it's the me right now, and
will still be me when I'm an old man. The
name won't change, but I will.*

Perhaps some day Jonah D. Krock will have an interesting life to write about. I hope so. The only thing I can say about my life so far is that it's a good beginning. I live with my father and mother. We move around a lot, so I've had a chance to see many cities and towns, and that has been a broadening experience.

I thought about what to put next that would really help me get into Fairlee, and I finally wrote:

When I write an autobiography, I hope to be able to say with pride that I am a Fairlee Boy.

I nearly threw up writing that last bit, but if it worked it was worth it.

That was just one page, and there were about a hundred pages to go. I had to do it and I had to do it now, and I had to do it right. The Fairlee Questionnaire was ruining my whole summer. I just had to get into that school. It was a boarding school, and that meant I'd be living away from my parents, and that was the main reason I had to get in. Not that my parents are terrible people or anything. They're very nice, as parents go, but they've got these screwy ideas. We don't have very much in common, as a matter of fact.

For instance, there are only three things in my life that I need to make me happy. One, watching television. Two, eating what I like. Three, not having to exercise every second. So, you can see I'm just a plain regular guy. It's my parents who are really weird. My mother is a health nut. She's got this notion that certain foods are terrific and certain other foods are terrible, and guess which is which. She thinks that anything that has just one tiny calorie in it is poison. So we never have anything to eat, just vegetables and stuff.

And my father—he's okay, I guess, but he's one of these super-energetic guys who thinks everybody else, mainly me, has got to be athletic, too. It's a real drag.

Well, all that's pretty crummy, as you see, but I haven't come to the worst part. You won't believe this: both my parents believe that when school starts television should stop. No television from September on! Even weekends. It's like saying "Don't breathe." The way they *talk* about television proves that they've been reading articles against it instead of watching it. Dad says things like "Your watching has grown from an occasional indulgence to a distressing habit, from a distressing habit to a dangerous addiction."

You can see what I mean about their being oddballs. To make absolutely positively sure that I don't sneak in five minutes of television after school starts, they said they'd get rid of the set in September. So of course I have to get out of this apartment and into that school.

Fairlee doesn't take just anybody, even if you've got good grades and even if you can afford it, and it's a very expensive school. They don't just look at your Previous School Record, they look at the Whole Boy.

Not wanting to be around my parents every second was one reason for wanting to go to Fairlee.

The other reason was something my parents didn't know anything about, something that I found out from the Fairlee representative. He had come to call on us one night to sell us on Fairlee. Those representatives probably get paid extra for every boy they can talk into going to Fairlee, so they really try hard.

I wasn't looking forward very much to his visit because it meant I had to miss some good programs. And I had to get out of my blue jeans and sneakers and into that stupid suit with a shirt and tie.

Everything about the Fairlee representative was round, even his name, which was Mr. Bowl, only he spelled it Bole, I found out later. In fact he looked exactly like the way I'd always drawn people, a series of various sizes of circles arranged to look like a body.

Mr. Bole had brought slides and a projector and catalogues and stuff with him, and after a little pep talk about Fairlee and what a great school it was, he set up the projector and showed about a million slides of the school. I'd never even *seen* Fairlee, and I was tired of it already.

He kept talking while he was showing the slides, about how he used to go there and how he wished he was a boy again, with a whole Fairlee Day stretching ahead of him. I kept thinking of all the television programs I was missing and wondering how many slides there were to go. Dad and Mom were saying things like "Oh, very nice," and "Lovely," very polite and bored. I know they were thinking how lucky they were they didn't have to go there.

After I'd missed three good TV programs, Mr. Bole came to the end of the slides. Mom and Dad hadn't said very much for the last couple dozen, and I guessed they'd probably dozed off. As soon as the lights were on, Mom blinked and jumped up and said, "Let's have some cookies and coffee, shall we?"

I didn't look forward to more of Mr. Bole, but I looked forward to the cookies. We never had cookies around, as I've explained. They were my favorite kind, chocolate chip and homemade. I knew Mom hadn't made them—naturally, she never did make stuff like that. I figured she'd bought them at a bake sale at the hospital or something.

Anyway, she shot me a meaningful glance as I helped myself to three right off the bat. Mom's very good at meaningful glances. Having the cookies had sort of made up for the dumb evening even if I *had* missed three programs.

Mr. Bole said, "Before I go, I'd like to have a man-to-man talk with Jonah, here, if that's all right." I groaned, but not so it showed. One more TV program down the drain.

After my parents had excused themselves (Mom took the cookie plate along with her, and I could hear the garbage disposal grinding them up), Mr. Bole put his round fingers on his round legs and leaned forward.

"Parents," he said, blinking behind his round glasses. "Sometimes they don't like us to have fattening foods. Believe me, I know just how you feel, Jonah, just exactly how you feel." So he'd seen that meaningful glance of my mother's.

He put a finger to his lips and whispered, "Mum's the word, Jonah, mum's the word. What I am about to tell you must be strictly between ourselves."

I nodded. "Sure."

"Fairlee has rather different ideas. For instance, every single room is equipped with its own refrigerator. A small refrigerator, but room enough for the things a boy loves. Ice cream, popsicles, fudge bars, chocolate-covered ice cream sticks—" I stared at him.

"We believe that every Fairlee boy should be able to eat what he wants. The theory behind this is that if it wasn't good for you, your body wouldn't crave it, right?"

"Right," I said. All of a sudden I liked Mr. Bole a lot more than I had.

"You can see why this is something we don't tell parents," said Mr. Bole, shrugging his shoulders. "Our program is based on the latest research. Parents—laymen—can't be expected to know all that the Fairlee staff and researchers know."

I nodded.

He examined his nails. "There's something else about Fairlee," he said. "There's a television set in every room, not a large set, but nevertheless a television set, color, of course. And no hours, no rules about watching and not watching. We at Fairlee believe that television is a part of a Fairlee boy's education. We believe it *helps* study habits."

Hey, this guy was terrific! He kept talking, I kept listening.

"We have discovered that a student watching cartoons or The Late Late Show while studying actually learns more than his counterpart, studying without television."

He sighed and leaned back. "I felt you should know all this, Jonah, before making your final choice of schools."

"Oh, I'm really glad you told me," I said.

"Remember, mum's the word. I don't like to keep these facts away from the parents of our new boys, but this is best at the outset. Later, of course, they will see that our methods work, they will see that you are a happier, healthier, more adjusted boy." He chuckled. "My own parents would never have let me attend Fairlee had they suspected I would have all the ice cream and candy I wanted, watch all the television I liked. Of course, later they discovered the wisdom of the Fairlee Way. So, too, will your parents, afterwards. But we won't tell them yet, will we?"

"I won't breathe a word," I promised.

"The important thing now is for you to fill out the questionnaire which I will leave with you. They're very, very fussy at Admissions about the questionnaire. If they're not satisfied with your answers, they will not accept your application. So try, Jonah, really try your best. Here's one hint that might be useful. They look for *sincerity* in their applicant."

Of course I'd try. I really *had* to get in. No matter what.

I could hardly get to sleep that night because I was excited about maybe going to Fairlee and worried about filling in the questionnaire the right way. I could hear Dad busy running in place. The push-ups would be next, and tomorrow morning it would all start all over again. Talk about dangerous addiction!

2 · You Make Your Friends, I'll Make Mine

Well, I'd finished the first part of the Fairlee Questionnaire, and I needed a candy bar more than I'd ever needed one before. Dinner was a long time away.

I knew there was a drugstore up at the corner and a grocery store in the next block. That's about all I knew about this neighborhood because we'd just moved. We were always moving.

I walked out to the kitchen. Mom was fussing around, rearranging the kitchen drawers. She was still unpacking the kitchen stuff and deciding where things should go. This was about the tenth time she'd changed everything around. She wanted to get stuff arranged as conveniently as possible so she could spend the least possible time in the kitchen.

"I'm going down to the lobby to check the mail," I told her. "Want me to pick up any groceries? Any lo-cal celery? Skim milk?"

Mom shook her head. "Thanks just the same. I've got everything we need."

That meant she had a good supply of spinach, cauliflower, okra, and yogurt.

"I met a very nice woman at that bridge party yesterday," said Mom. "She has a son just your age. I told her—"

I groaned. Parents think that if they like someone, *that* someone has to have a perfect son.

"Nice parents usually have terrible kids," I said.

"They live right in the next block. It wouldn't hurt to try," said Mom.

I shook my head. "That's even worse," I told her. I knew what would happen if I didn't nip this in the bud. Mom would invite this new friend over and ask her to bring her son, and I wouldn't be able to escape. Ever.

"Look, Mom," I said, being really firm. "Every

single place I've ever been, at school, or at camp, or any of the apartment buildings where we've lived, somebody latches onto me for a friend, and then he turns out to be a real moron or a kleptomaniac or a pyromaniac or some other kind of maniac, and then everybody sees me with him and figures I'm a real creep, too."

Mom nodded. Maybe she was listening to me, maybe she was figuring out where to put the steak knives, maybe she was wondering which day to invite this friend and her creepy son over to meet me.

"You make your friends, I'll make mine," I said.

She turned around and was just about to launch into Monologue 23, which was how I was turning into a television hermit, and how I would have to be more sociable and how I would have to—

Before she could get started, I said, "Back in a few, have a quick errand to run," and escaped.

I got my candy bar. In fact, to tell the truth, I got three candy bars. I ate two on the way back to the apartment building and one walking through the lobby, and I realized I was hungry again.

I got in the elevator. Someone was already in there but I couldn't see much of him because he was carrying this enormous paper bag, and all I could see were his arms and legs, and that wasn't very exciting. He was kind of wheezing or coughing.

His huge brown paper bag was filled with groceries. At least there were bananas on top, so I figured out that all of it was probably groceries.

He couldn't see over the top of the bag, and I guess he thought he was alone in the elevator. I had dashed in just as the door was closing. He did the wheezing bit for a while, and then he started talking to himself. It was a kind of chant, and at first I thought it was a foreign language (which wouldn't have surprised me since he looked as if he could have come from Mars or somewhere), but the more I listened the more words I could pick out, and I could finally tell it was a shopping list:

Lettuce, tomatoes, Ritz crackers and cheese,
Puffed Puffies, ice cream, frozen spinach and
*   peas,*
Bananas and tuna and macaroneeeees.

I'm a pretty quiet breather, so he didn't know I was on board until the elevator stopped at fourteen, and I started to get out. He started to get out, too, so we bumped into each other, and the groceries fell all over the place. When the elevator door closed, most of the groceries were on the hall floor, and the bananas were in the elevator. "Yipes!" he said. He stared at the elevator door, and his eyes practically bulged right out of his head. He started to blink, I guess to keep them from falling out.

"They've gone up in the elevator!" he shouted. It wasn't exactly a shout, it was more of a screech. I couldn't see why bananas were all that important unless you were starving to death, and I decided that maybe he was, he was pretty emaciated and all. "Emaciated" is one of my new words. I'm trying to build up my vocabulary.

He was standing there kind of gasping and staring at the elevator indicator. He was sort of scrawny and had about a million pimples, two million if you counted the ones on his arms and legs. If I had that many pimples, I wouldn't go around in shorts and T-shirts. I'd wear long blue jeans and sleeves that came down to my wrists, and I'd wear big dark glasses that would cover most of my face, and I'd have long hair that would cover my forehead. And then when I was old enough, if I hadn't outgrown the pimples by then, I'd grow a moustache and a beard and sideburns and all that, and the only thing anybody would see of me would be my mouth. And if I had teeth like his, I wouldn't open it very often.

I really shouldn't criticize his teeth, because mine aren't all that great, at least they weren't the last time I saw them, which was about a million years ago before I began wearing braces. But at least my teeth, the last time I saw them, were white. Not real white, not pearly white, but anyone would know at a glance that white was the color they were closest to. This guy's teeth weren't white, or gray, or even yellow, but some funny color you don't usually associate with teeth. I looked away from them and up to the dial above the elevator. The elevator (and the bananas) were on the eighteenth floor.

I sprang into action. For me, action is usually spending the least possible amount of energy because I am a very sedentary person, according to my parents.

Anyway, I reached over and pressed the down button, which wasn't all that athletic, but it was more than he was doing, anyway, and I said, "Don't worry, we'll just get that crazy old elevator down here with those bananas."

I was trying to be real calm so he wouldn't explode or anything. He did anyway.

"It may be too late!" he screeched. "They'll die! They'll die!"

I tried to think of something soothing to say. Fortunately on television the night before there had been somebody dealing with an emotional crisis situation like this on the program. Well, not like this of course, nothing could be, but anyway an emotional crisis thing, a kidnaped baby, as a matter of fact.

"There, there, now," I said, using the phrase that had worked so successfully on television the night before.

I thought he was going to jump right out of his pimply skin, and what a mess that would be. He stared at the elevator indicator, and I glanced up again. Still on eighteen.

He started wheezing and coughing. "Don't worry," I said, being as soothing as possible, "those bananas won't die up there. They last several days. It's an interesting thing about bananas," I went on, watching to see if he was going to faint or go into spasms or what. "Do you know, for instance, that you should never keep bananas in the refrigerator? And the reason for that is—"

He interrupted with a kind of high-pitched groan or gulp. "It isn't coming down, it isn't coming down! They'll die!"

Talk about bananas, he was going bananas right in front of my eyes. I looked down the corridor. Nothing but doors, six of them. One of them was the door to our apartment, one must be the door to his, which left four, which is about all I know about math. Maybe there was a doctor behind one, or a psychiatrist or something.

Meantime, I'd have to handle the situation, which was a sticky one as far as I was concerned, because I'd never run into anyone with irrational behavior like this before, except of course on TV, and I was worried because the next thing that happens is that they hit you over the head or something. He was turning white or else his pimples were turning pinker, it was hard to say, but he had this kind of pickled look on his face.

I kept trying the soothing bit, which was the best I could think of.

"They looked pretty healthy to me," I said, reassuringly. "A few brown spots, but you know in bananas that is not an alarming sign, just a nice normal indication that—"

"I'm going up," he announced. At first I thought he said he was *throwing* up, which wouldn't have been surprising. He turned and headed for the stairs.

"Hey, wait!" I shouted. There was no telling what this nut might do, off chasing his bananas. "What about those groceries?" I called. "What about the asparagus? What about the peas? Don't leave them here alone," I yelled, as he threw open the door to the stairway. "What about the Puffed Puffies?" I shouted. "Don't you even care about them?"

The door to the stairway swung shut, and I stood there, surrounded by canned tuna fish and macaroni and ice cream and wondered what I should do. Rush to our telephone and call the hospital? Race after this weirdo? Or wait for him to return with the ailing bananas?

I stood there watching the unmoving dial of

the elevator indicator. Eighteen.

Then it started down.

I am not a fast decision maker, and by the time I had sorted out my options, the elevator door opened, and he bolted out, holding the bananas in one hand and a little container from the deli in the other. He pushed past me, carrying the bananas aloft like a torch and started running down the corridor. "They're alive!" he screeched. "But we have to hurry! I think Emily's dying!"

I'd never heard of anybody who named bananas, and I just stood there watching him as he ran down the corridor, holding the bananas up in the air. "Hurry!" he called over his shoulder. "There's no time to lose!"

I started to pick up the spilled groceries, and he yelled, "Hurry, they'll die, Emily's in real trouble!"

I ran over to him and he sputtered, "Key! Key! In my left pocket!"

I reached in his nearest pocket.

"Left, left, left!" he screeched. Finally, I found the key and got it in the lock and opened the door. I mean that sounds easy and usually it *is* easy, find key, put in lock, turn, open, but under these circumstances it was very, very difficult.

As soon as the door was open he pushed ahead of me.

"Kitchen!" he called. "Turn on the water! Hurry!"

I ran to the kitchen sink and turned on the water. "Hot or cold?" I yelled. That shows how rattled I was. Usually I don't get rattled easily.

"Cold, cold!" He was rushing around like a raving maniac, and there was a lot of clattering and thumping as he rummaged madly in the kitchen cupboards. What was he looking for? Maybe a thermometer for the bananas, maybe a towel to wrap them in, maybe a hammer to attack me with.

I was still determined to be as soothing as possible, so I said, "Emily is a very nice name. What are the names of the rest of the bananas?"

He was so busy rattling things around, pulling things out of the kitchen cupboards like a wild man, that he didn't answer. Maybe he had more bananas hidden in there, maybe he'd turn on me with a butcher knife or something, so I still was very, very calm, and I said, "There now, the water's nice and cold, let's put our heads under it, okay? I don't know about you, but I always like to put my head under some nice cold water if things aren't going along too well, and—"

He dragged out a big mixing bowl and yelled, "Fill it! Fill it!" I figured he wanted to dunk his head in it but he shouted, "We've got to get them in fast or they'll die!"

Oh, so we were back to the bananas again. They were right on the counter next to me, so as soon as the bowl started filling up with water, I reached over for them and plunked them in. "There," I said, "everything's going to be fine now. Look at Emily. She's perking up already!"

He gave me a cold stare. "What are you, some kind of nut or something?" he asked. He tossed the bananas out of the bowl and reached for the deli carton. He opened the carton and dumped in some little tropical fish, guppies or something. He put his head down to look at them until his nose was practically in the bowl.

He breathed a sigh of relief. "They'll be okay now until I get them into the aquarium," he said. "The water has spilled out of the carton. These new fish would have died if I hadn't got them in the bowl, and I'd already named them. Emily, Thorax, and Sybil."

He gazed at them and breathed on them for a minute and then turned to me.

"You've got a real thing about bananas, right?" he asked. "You should probably see a psychiatrist. Sometimes these things have a way of getting out of hand, even a seemingly innocent affection for bananas. Having strange fixations is a perfectly normal manifestation of puberty, of course, and food fixations are relatively common, but—"

Well, I wasn't going to hang around just to get insulted, so I started for the door. I'd helped him save his stupid fish, and he wasn't even going to thank me. Not that I do things just for the thanks I get, but after all it had been a very traumatic experience for me. For him, sure, but they were his fish, not mine, so he should be the one to have the headaches, not me, an innocent bystander.

He followed me out of the apartment. "I've got to pick up the groceries," he said. "I'll have to make two or three trips. If you help me we can do it in one. Then we can have some ice cream with chocolate sauce and butterscotch sauce and peanuts."

I hesitated for one billionth of a second.

"Okay," I said.

"My name's Goober," he said. "What's yours?"

"Moose," I lied. Then I helped him pick up all those cans of tuna fish and canned spaghetti and ice cream, and we went back to his apartment.

3 · Who's Got Problems?

Goober got out the syrups and nuts and that marshmallow stuff, and we started to fix ourselves sundaes.

He leaned over to pick up the bananas. "We could have a banana split," he suggested. Then he frowned and pursed his lips. "Unless of course you don't want to eat them. Maybe you just want to have them around where you can see them, take care of them, put them in bowls of water for their baths and everything."

"A banana split would be fine," I said. "I don't have a thing about bananas, I thought you did."

Goober nodded seriously. "That's very understandable. We all like to think that others share our own problems."

I stopped trying to straighten him out and just concentrated on making a banana split.

He didn't say anything else for a few minutes. I was to find out that silences are very rare with Goober. "Raising tropical fish is my hobby," said Goober. "What's yours?"

Actually, I didn't have a hobby, unless you count watching television, and nobody does, so I pretended I didn't hear him.

We took our banana splits into the living room because the kitchen was all over groceries and the dining room table was all over books and papers and charts. The chairs and couches in the living room were covered with unopened boxes from some shop or store, so we sat on the floor. It didn't seem to be a very well-organized apartment. I wondered who lived with him and whether it was parents or guardians. He seemed to be the guardian type. I didn't want to ask, though. I try not to ask questions since I hate answering them so much myself.

We started to eat our banana splits.

"You live on this floor?" he asked. He had chocolate syrup all over his face. If there's anything I hate it's a sloppy eater.

"Not exactly," I said cautiously. Living on the same floor with this bird was going to make my life pretty hard. I'd be stuck with him all summer and for all I knew the rest of my life. I'd have to lie a little to keep from getting tangled up.

"Not exactly," he repeated, licking his spoon. "What's that supposed to mean?"

"Well, actually, it's kind of hard to explain," I said, stalling for time and trying to think up something to say. To tell you the truth, lying comes pretty easy to me. "My father is the janitor of the building. There are ten of us kids, and we don't have enough beds to go around, so we take turns sleeping in the elevator. It's really a nice arrangement."

He started to say something. I could see his mouth opening and showing all the ice cream mushing around in there, so I hurried on. "I know what you're going to say. You're going to say that sounds monotonous, but you'd be surprised the people you meet in the elevator. And you always know what the weather is like because everyone says something like "Nice day, isn't it?" or "Some rain we're getting" or "That's sure a sharp wind" so you really learn a lot. A lot more, for instance, than if you lived in an apartment on the fourteenth floor. That way you don't meet anybody."

"Thirteenth," said Goober, taking another bite of his banana split.

"Thirteenth what?" I asked.

"Floor. It's called fourteenth because most people are too superstitious to live on the thirteenth. There isn't any floor that's called thirteenth. This is it, but it's named fourteenth."

He explained all this very slowly and carefully as if I was some little kid or something.

"For instance," he went on, poking at his banana split with his spoon, "this apartment is called 1410 but it really should be called 1310."

"I get it, I get it," I said.

"Haven't you noticed that before?" he asked. "Spending so much time in the elevator, I would think you'd have noticed that there is no floor that is named the thirteenth floor. Of course you may not be an observant person. I happen to be an unusually observant person."

"Oh, I am, too, usually," I said. "Usually, I'm unusually observant. It's just that I'm so busy observing the people who get on and off the elevator that I don't notice anything else. Anything but their groceries, of course. I always watch for the groceries."

Goober glanced over at me and then approached his banana split again.

"I get to meet lots of interesting people and interesting groceries," I went on. "Like, for instance, I met you today." I kept talking so he wouldn't. "I always wait for someone to get on the elevator with a bag of groceries and hope that in the bag will be a bunch of bananas. As you've discovered, I really like to look at bananas and make sure they're safe and comfortable and happy. And they're usually on the top of the bag, so I can always see them. Now if I liked tuna fish or something like that, it would be much more difficult because tuna fish cans are usually on the bottom."

He opened his mouth to say something but it was full of ice cream so I talked on. "I have this invention for transparent grocery bags. It would really be great for guys like me who like to see the groceries, not just wonder about what's in that brown paper bag and could it be a can of mushroom soup or a box of Puffed Puffies or what."

He started to squash his banana up with the chocolate sauce and all that other stuff. That way it's just like some goopy paste, it isn't like a banana split at all, when you can see and taste and feel all the different textures, so I said, "You shouldn't mash it all up that way."

Goober said, "It doesn't hurt the banana any more than chewing it, you know. Besides, I'm not convinced that bananas feel anything at all, in spite of your own convictions about it."

He went out to the kitchen and came back with two glasses of milk. "My father will be very, very interested," he said as he handed me my milk. "He loves things like that."

"Things like what?" I asked.

"Oh, screwy things, you know, like having a thing for elevators, or bananas. He isn't a psychiatrist himself, you understand. He's a broker. But he's very into reading about oddballs. He's got some theory about people like you. He thinks you're tuned into a different wavelength. You see things and hear things that normal people don't. That's why you all seem so odd to the rest of us."

"Your father really has us figured out, huh?" I asked.

"He doesn't pass judgment or anything," Goober went on. "He just observes. For instance, he wouldn't hold it against you about the bananas. He'd be interested, of course, but he wouldn't judge."

Goober blinked at the mess he had made of his banana split. It looked just like mud. He ran his spoon around the side of the dish to get the last ugly drops.

I didn't want to, but I started to look at his teeth. I wondered if maybe the funny color was because he ate a lot of blueberries, for example. Or—

"You wear braces," he said. I guess my looking at his teeth must have made him think about mine. "How long have you worn them?" he asked, staring with absorption at my mouth.

"Meeth yuus," I said through buttoned lips.

"I didn't mean to ask you when you had your mouth full," he said. He waited an appropriate interval so he could be sure I'd have swallowed, and then he said again, "How long have you worn braces?"

It's a funny thing about questions, even if you

don't want to answer, you have to. It's like waiting for the second shoe to drop, it's as if there's a balance that's out of kilter. Question, answer, question, answer, sunrise, sunset, and unanswered questions create a kind of gap or gulp in the rhythm of things, and everything's out of joint. So I said, still keeping my lips shut, "Meeth yuus" again. "Actually, I was born with braces," I went on. "I'm a wave of the future. In the future people won't have any teeth at all, just braces, because all their food will be very, very soft, maybe just even pills. Teeth will be an anachronism. An anachronism is—"

"The reason I asked," he interrupted, "was the fact that you have worn braces for many years might be a very important factor in your present problems."

"Who's got problems?" I asked. "I have no problems."

"That's the most flagrant symptom, of course," said Goober, "thinking that you yourself have no problems. My father will be very, very interested."

I pictured that his father was probably an older, taller, skinnier, uglier Goober, and I didn't want to meet him and answer his questions.

"Well, I've got to go," I said. "We usually have dinner pretty early. Thanks for the banana split."

I'm very good about the social amenities. My parents drilled all that into me from the time I was born so it's a kind of automatic reflex. I don't mean that I deserve credit for it or anything, but at least I say thank you and stuff like that.

"I thought you handled the whole thing about the banana splits very well," he said, "considering your hangups about bananas."

He was pretty good about the social bit, too, I could see. He'd probably gone to a school where they taught you all that or else he had parents (or guardians) who paid attention.

He followed me out to the elevator so he could watch the indicator to see what floor I got off. When I got in I pressed the button for nineteen just to fool him. When I got to nineteen I walked down to my own floor, fourteen (thirteen). If I judged him right, he'd go to the mailboxes in the lobby and look at the names of the people on nineteen and try to figure out which one was me.

If I worked things out, I'd never have to see

him again. It would take some maneuvering, since we lived on the same floor, but I could do it.

Mom was still fussing around in the kitchen when I got back to our apartment. She'd hung up a huge calorie chart on the wall. I noticed that one banana was 130 calories. One half cup of raw cabbage was ten.

"I met this really screwy kid who lives on our floor," I said, opening the refrigerator door and closing it again with a big sigh so she'd maybe notice and feel sorry for me.

"Good," said Mom. "See, it's not so hard to make friends if you try."

"He is not a friend, and it isn't good, it's terrible," I said. "He's got some weird ideas. He thinks I'm weird."

"That shows he's very perceptive," said Mom.

"Besides, he's a very nervous person," I told her.

"Who isn't?" she asked, arranging all the spoons in a drawer. "He probably watches too much television. It's bad for your nervous system."

That was her way of nagging me about watching too much television. "Dinner's almost ready, so don't get started watching some program."

Since I'd just had the banana split, I knew I wouldn't be able to eat. "I'm not too hungry," I said. I knew dinner was going to be something like calves' liver and cauliflower.

"Good," said Mom. "Do you want to ask your new friend over for supper? He could have your share."

I sighed. "He is not a new friend. He's not anything. Just a nut who lives on this floor. I don't want to get involved with this creep. If you want to know something that's hard on your nervous system, it's this oddball."

"Well, if he lives on this floor, you're bound to see a lot of him," said Mom, putting spices on the spice rack. "You might as well be friends."

"No way," I said firmly. "I'm figuring out a system so I won't ever run into him again. He's a very excitable person."

I wandered into the living room and turned on the television set.

"Don't forget to fill out that questionnaire," called Mom. "You'd better do that before you turn on TV." There was something about my conversations with Mom that made me sigh a lot. I sighed. As if I could forget the questionnaire.

I worked on it while I watched a pretty good program about some cops-and-robber chase. I'd filled in all the things like name and age and height and weight, truthfully. Well, I put my weight down as a few pounds less than it was because I was going to lose a lot of weight between now and fall, probably.

WHAT IS YOUR FAVORITE VACATION?

Actually, my favorite vacation was three years ago when my parents took one and left me at home with a Mrs. Sneedly. She was the best baby-sitter I'd ever had. She was a television *addict*. We'd watch the morning cartoons and game shows and soap operas and afternoon movies and reruns and situation comedies and late late shows.

She didn't like to cook, for fear she'd miss a program, so we had lots of frozen TV dinners and frozen cakes and pies. We'd eat when we felt like it, which was about all the time. Sometimes we'd have cake and ice cream first thing in the morning. Sometimes we had it three meals a day.

Well, when my parents came back two weeks later, it was a real culture shock. I felt like running away to join the circus—or Mrs. Sneedly.

Vacation. To me a vacation isn't a vacation because my parents are always with me. What would be good would be a vacation from them. Just for a change of scene.

Well, back to the questionnaire.

WHAT IS YOUR FAVORITE VACATION?

My favorite type of vacation is traveling with my family, sharing new sights, new sounds, new adventures, new insights.

I like a vacation that expands my horizons, that challenges me, that broadens me, that sends me back to my regular routine with a new perspective.

· It had taken me three programs plus supper with Mom to get that far. Now I was really hungry again. Mom was taking a shower and washing her hair. I decided I'd have time to sneak out and get a candy bar, but when I opened the door Goober was standing at the elevator. I tried ten minutes later, and he was still there, sitting on the floor in front of it, picking his nose. Waiting for me, probably. Well, he could wait. I looked around in the kitchen cupboards but there wasn't anything but canned salmon and stuff like that. I was really hungry for something sweet, and I was really mad at Goober for standing—or sitting—in my way. I wasn't going to leave the apartment while he was there. I waited and looked again. Goober was still there. I opened the door a tiny crack and watched him for a couple of minutes. Every once in a while he'd stand up and push the elevator button. The elevator would come, the doors would open, he'd peer inside, and then he'd just keep sitting there, picking his nose.

I'd have to forget about going out. When I went to bed all I could think of was that creep sitting in the hall, keeping me from my candy bar.

4 · The Banana Boy

That next week I worked out a pretty foolproof system for keeping out of Goober's way, or keeping him out of mine. I never left our apartment without first making sure he wasn't in the hall. Then I'd rush for the stairs. That way he couldn't find me standing there waiting for the elevator.

I'd sneak down the stairs to the next floor or the next. Then I'd go to the elevator and press the down button, watching the elevator indicator to make sure the elevator didn't stop at fourteen (thirteen) on the way to get me. That way I knew it would be safe to get on without running into him.

It worked. Luck was on my side, I thought.

47

Then one day I was standing there on twelve, watching the elevator indicator, when suddenly the stairway door opened, and Goober peered out at me.

"I knew I'd find you eventually on one floor or another," he said. "I thought you lived on nineteen."

See how well I had him figured? He *had* watched to see what floor I'd get off on. I tried to keep my sigh from showing. It was like trying to smother a sneeze.

"I live on thirteen, actually," I said. "Everybody thinks there's no thirteen, but there is, and that's where the janitor's apartment is. You can't get to it on the elevator, or on this stairway. There's a special stairway that not everybody knows about."

"What I wanted to ask you was if you could—" Goober started to interrupt.

I knew he was going to ask me some dumb favor, so I kept talking. "The way you get to the special stairway is that in one of these apartments on twelve is this one door that looks like a closet door but it's really the door to the stairway to thirteen, where we live."

"Since you're not doing anything right now, maybe you could—" interrupted Goober.

"The reason we have to keep it so secret," I went on, "is that otherwise everybody would be knocking on our door all the time, asking my father to fix their faucets or their window shades or their doorknobs or something. We wouldn't have any privacy at all. And we're a family that loves our privacy. And—"

"Hey," Goober said, interrupting fast to keep me from interrupting *him* again, "want to come up and help me move my aquarium? It takes two. Otherwise, I'll have to drain the whole thing and transfer the fish and everything, and it would take hours."

See? I was right. He *had* wanted to ask me some dumb favor. He didn't even know me and here he was already asking me to help move his old aquarium. "Why can't you just leave it where it is?" I asked.

"Because it's right next to the air conditioner, and the fish will catch cold. They might even get pneumonia." Goober screwed his face around to one of his odd and anxious expressions.

"I'm not all that strong," I said, stalling for

time, trying to think up excuses. "I might drop it or something."

"We could have a banana split afterwards," he said cagily.

I considered. I hadn't had much breakfast, I'm not a big breakfast eater, and the banana split sounded pretty good. "Is your father home?" I asked. I didn't want to meet his father, one Goober was enough.

"Nobody's home, Dad's at the office, my mother's at the optometrist, and I've got to get the aquarium moved right away. Come on, we've got to hurry."

"Why don't you shut off the air conditioner?" I asked, knowing that I was fighting a losing battle.

"I'm allergic to warm weather," he said, starting to wheeze and cough to show me how sickly he was.

I decided it probably wouldn't kill me to give him a hand with the aquarium, seeing that he really liked those goopy fish of his. And I could use that banana split. So I followed him up the stairs to fourteen (thirteen) and into his apartment. The same stuff was all over the place—the papers and books on the dining room table, and the boxes on the living room furniture. Or maybe it was different books and different boxes. Anyway, it looked pretty much the same.

I followed Goober into his room. It had to be his room—there was a big aquarium on one shelf, an unmade bed, and piles of clothes everywhere. That made me like him better. I'd thought he'd be one of those super-neat guys that are a pain in the neck. Goober was certainly a pain in the neck, but at least he was messy. That was something on his side.

He had it worked out ahead of time how we were going to move the aquarium. He'd already put tables between where the aquarium was and where it was going to be, so we could set it down three different times. We moved it to the first table. It was pretty heavy and the water started sloshing around.

"Maybe they'll get seasick," I said. "Then they'll throw up. Maybe we should leave it where it was."

"If you have to throw up," said Goober anxiously, "try to wait until after we get the aquarium moved."

Goober heard only about one word in ten, unless it was his own voice.

After we got the aquarium as far as the third table, Goober leaned over to examine it. "Too much stress here at the seam," he announced. "Got to get some putty or we'll have a leak on our hands." He started running around the room, banging drawers open and shut, and finally he said, "I've got to run over to the pet shop for some putty, I'll be right back."

He zoomed out of the apartment, slamming the door behind him. I watched the fish for a while, but that wasn't very exciting, so I wandered around Goober's room, and that wasn't very exciting, either. A messy room isn't all that great to wander around in, especially if it's a pretty small room, so I went into the living room and wandered around in there, waiting for Goober to come back with the putty. I could have been working on the questionnaire or watching television.

After about ten hours I heard someone knocking at the apartment door. I knew it must be Goober, and that he'd forgotten his key.

I opened the door and this tall, thin lady wearing big dark glasses walked in.

"I couldn't even find the keyhole, darling," she said. "Absolutely ghastly drops in my eyes, plus these wicked glasses, I can't see a *thing*. I *told* him I didn't want drops."

She walked into the living room. "Find me my white coat, there's a love, no telling what I might end up with since I'm practically blind as a bat, dearest boy, blind as a bat, and I'm having lunch at Helen Barsley's. Her apartment is always ten degrees below *freezing*, no wonder she's always coming down with colds, she lives in the arctic zone. Why I said I'd go I can't fathom. The white coat, darling, in the closet."

I picked out a white coat from the hall closet and handed it to her.

"By the way, dearest boy," she said, "your father told me about your friend, the janitor's son? The banana boy? Really, darling, I wouldn't encourage that friendship if I were you, he sounds as if he'd be a very, very unhealthy influence. Just because you feel sorry for someone, that doesn't mean you have to have him for a friend. I'm sure there are many, many nice boys in this building with whom you would have much, much more in common. Boys who share your own background, your own ideals, darling. This boy sounds very, very odd."

She threw the coat over her shoulders like a cape.

"I absolutely dread Helen Barsley's luncheons. She always has creamed things on toast—soft little mysterious things—very, very difficult to identify. The most *dreadful* possibilities come into your mind as you're swallowing them."

She smiled in my direction as she opened the door. "Be sure to eat now, dearest love."

I hate people who criticize other peoples' mothers, so I won't say anything, but I was really glad she wasn't *my* mother.

I meandered around some more, looking at the paintings on the walls, all very modern, the kind you think you could do yourself if you wanted to, and finally Goober came back with the stuff for the aquarium, and then finally we had the thing moved to where he wanted it.

I had really earned that banana split. While we were making them, Goober asked, "How many brothers and sisters did you say you have?"

"Nine," I said. "There are ten counting me, so that means I've got nine siblings. Siblings means brothers or sisters."

"I know," said Goober. "I would have used that word to begin with if I had thought you'd understand it. That's pretty good for your age." He scrunched his face into another ugly version of his own. "The reason I ask how many is that when I talked to my father about you, he felt that some of your symptoms might be due to the overcrowded nest syndrome. Insecurity, fighting for attention, the usual manifestations of—"

"He's probably right," I said, counting the peanuts on my banana split. Twenty seven.

We carried our banana splits into the living room and sat on the floor.

"Sometimes it takes an outsider to see things objectively. Actually, I feel that I may have helped you," announced Goober, starting to mash up his banana. "You are now able to eat bananas without any qualms at all. When I first met you, remember, you were very nervous about bananas."

"Don't think I don't have problems, still," I said. "Just because I'm having this banana split right now in comparative peace and calm doesn't mean that I'm always that way. I'm suffering inside."

"That's very understandable," said Goober, stirring his squashed-up banana. "But now that you understand your problem you may find it easier to overcome it. Facing yourself is half the battle."

Think how old Goober would seem by the time he was thirty or forty or fifty, when he was a little old man *now.*

Looking at Goober, I began thinking about the rest of the Fairlee Questionnaire: WHAT ONE QUALITY DO YOU LOOK FOR IN A FRIEND BEYOND ALL OTHER QUALITIES?

Goober had a big mouthful of pulverized banana—in his mouth and on his face.

First of all, a friend should eat with his mouth closed.

He started to talk. I looked away.

"Actually, a lot of your problem stems from the fact that—"

I choose a friend for one reason: that he keep his analysis of my personality problems to himself.

I gulped down the rest of my banana split. I had to finish that questionnaire. What if I got it in late, just because I couldn't think of anything to say?

I hardly watched any TV that night. Just two or three programs that I couldn't miss. The rest of the time I worked on the questionnaire.

WHAT ONE QUALITY DO YOU LOOK FOR IN A FRIEND BEYOND ALL OTHER QUALITIES?

I look first of all for sincerity, because if a friend is sincere he is honest. A true friendship must be an honest one.

That one took me forever, and I wrote it about ten times before I got it right.

5 · It Has a Lot to Do with the Stars

I'd gone down to the lobby to check our mailbox. I always checked the mailbox every time I walked through the lobby, even if I'd just looked in it ten minutes before.

A voice behind me squawked, "Yipes! It finally came!"

I turned around. Goober was waving an envelope as if it was a flag. I moved away quickly from our mailbox so he couldn't see which one I'd been going to open.

His eyes darted from me to the envelope and back again. "Know what this is?" he asked. I shook my head.

"It's that thing I sent for. I've been waiting three weeks. All our mail is late because it's being forwarded here, see." His pimples glowed, his eyes bulged, his strange teeth shone darkly.

"What thing you sent for?" I asked cautiously.

He tore open the envelope. "Look!" he said, extracting from the envelope a pink sheet of paper. "It's my horoscope. My special one. I sent in for it. With the exact second of my birth and the exact place I was born. It's all very scientific, you know." He scowled briefly. He glanced at the pink sheet. "Very, very interesting," he muttered. "This will be very helpful."

"I didn't know you were interested in astrology," I said, edging farther away from our mailbox so that he wouldn't even have a clue to who I was or where I lived.

"I'm interested in everything," he said. "Later I can sort things out and select the few areas of interest that I want to concentrate on." He peered again at the pink sheet of paper. Then he squinted over at me. "I can send for a horoscope for you," he said. He reached in his pocket and took out a pencil stub. "Just give me your name and the exact moment of your birth and the exact place." Clever!

"I don't remember," I said.

"It only costs a quarter," he insisted.

"I'll ask my folks," I told him. "Maybe they'll remember. I'll let you know." I started edging away. He followed me.

"You'd learn a lot from a horoscope. You'd learn why you're different from other people. It has a lot to do with the stars. It might help you solve some of your problems."

I kept edging away, and he kept following, his face screwed up into an odd new arrangement. I'd never seen anyone who rearranged his features as often and with as little success as Goober.

I had to get rid of him some way. I walked over to the elevator. Politely I stood aside holding the door while he went in. I followed him, still holding the door open. Then I let it go and jumped out of the elevator quickly. "Forgot something! See you later!" I said as the door closed.

Victory. He still didn't know who I was or where I lived. But I knew my days were numbered.

I decided to walk all the way up to the fourteenth (thirteenth) floor to get the adrenalin out of my system. I'd have to work on the questionnaire today for sure. I sighed. If I wasn't worrying about Goober and getting away from him, I was worrying about the questionnaire. Right now it felt good to worry about the questionnaire because it kept my mind off Goober. It was like having a toothache and dropping a rock on your foot so you could forget about the toothache.

I finally made it up to our floor. I settled down in front of the television set with the questionnaire, puffing. The stairs—and the encounter with Goober—had nearly done me in.

One of the hardest parts was the section on HOBBIES. They'd left a lot of space to fill in, which meant they were expecting everyone to fill in a lot of stuff.

MY HOBBIES AND WHY I HAVE CHOSEN THEM.

I didn't have any hobbies. *Watching Television* wouldn't sound like a real Fairlee Boy.

I'd never needed hobbies before, but I needed some now. I'd decided the day before to say that one of my hobbies was reading, because that sounded intellectual. I'd figured out my reason for choosing that hobby:

> *Reading stimulates my mind and enables me to experience vicariously the lives of others. That in turn helps to enlarge my own intellectual horizons.*

I'd really worked on that one. I didn't add that all I read was comic books and murder mysteries.

Now sitting in front of the TV I read over that bit about reading. I didn't want to sound too intellectual—a Fairlee Boy is a Balanced Boy. So I needed something to balance the reading bit.

Suddenly I thought about Goober and his fish, and I put down *Raising Tropical Fish*. Actually, that was partly true, if it hadn't been for me Goober's fish would have died. But the reason I'd chosen that? I couldn't for the life of me decide. I read the catalogue one more time, hoping to get an inspiration.

There was a picture of Fairlee Boys standing around a dinner table with their eyes shut. I was pretty sure that they weren't all sleeping, so I figured they were saying grace or something.

Maybe I could throw in something about religion, or God, or both. Finally I wrote:

Learning about God's creatures enables me to understand and appreciate the many varied forms of life in this world.

I almost wrote *Amen* after that. It was the second time I'd used the word *enables,* but maybe they wouldn't notice. It sounded more intellectual than *helps.*

I wondered if two hobbies would be enough. Probably not for the well-rounded Fairlee Boy. There was still lots of space left.

I'd have to come up with a sport to make me *really* well rounded. I couldn't think of anything that I could safely put down, because whatever it was they'd expect me to play it if I ever got to Fairlee. I put the questionnaire away and concentrated on television. I get lots of my ideas from television. And sure enough. There was a commercial for some soft drink, and it had these two mountain climbers climbing up and up and finally reaching the top and finding this soft drink up there.

What about mountain climbing as my hobby? There weren't even any hills around Fairlee so they'd never find out whether I knew how to climb mountains or not. I thought about it for the next couple of programs, and I finally wrote down *Mountain Climbing* as my third hobby. And for my reason I wrote:

> *The challenge of a mountain is simply this: If it is there, I must get to the top. The mountain represents to me the best, the summit, of my own self. I want to attain whatever heights in me are possible.*

Wow. Maybe I'd poured it on a little too thick and gooey, but the way I figured it couldn't be too thick or too gooey for Fairlee. Any school that would have in its catalogue things like "Send us your boy today, and we'll send a man back to you tomorrow," and "With pride and strength and quiet joy I say, 'I am a Fairlee Boy,' " would be impressed by any phony mishmash I could come up with.

At least I'd finished the section on hobbies.

Reading
Raising Tropical Fish
Mountain Climbing

And I'd had to neglect my real one—watching television—just to dream up the phony ones. I'd have a lot of catching up to do once I'd mailed in the questionnaire.

6 · A Stroke of Genius

Mom had decided to have a bridge party. Since it was an afternoon party and since everyone always fixed dessert at the afternoon parties she went to, she figured that's what she'd better do.

"I wish I could serve raw carrots," she grumbled, leafing through a cookbook, her least favorite pastime. The party was to be the next day.

Suddenly I had an inspiration. "How about banana splits?" I asked. "I could get all the stuff and make them myself. Then you wouldn't have to bother."

"A stroke of genius," she said, laughing and closing the cookbook. "Banana splits it is, the fatter the better. A splurge." She looked at me thoughtfully. "One banana split can't hurt you," she said.

She gave me money to get the stuff, and I started off for the store, automatically remembering to walk down a couple of floors before I got on the elevator. I hadn't seen Goober for a while and with any luck and planning I wouldn't have to see him again. Because every single time he appeared it was an adrenalin-producing experience that took me hours to adjust to and to recover from.

I came back to the apartment building with two huge paper bags filled with chocolate and vanilla and strawberry ice cream and butter-scotch sauce and chocolate syrup and marshmallow goop and lots of nuts and maraschino cherries and bunches and bunches of bananas. I thought I'd have to make two trips but I finally managed. Talk about athletes! You should have seen those enormous bags. I'm not very strong but I'm a very good balancer.

Just as I was getting into the lobby elevator, shifting the bags, some smart alec little kid with a runny nose was getting out.

"Push your floor for you?" he asked. I nodded. "Fourteen, thanks," I said.

He pushed every single button on the elevator and sped off, calling over his shoulder, "Have a nice trip, Dip, have a nice ride, Snide, have a nice time, Grime, have a nice journey, Nerny," and stuff like that. If I caught him I'd shake him till his teeth rattled, but I couldn't run after him now.

So here I was on an elevator that was going to stop at every single floor. Doors open, long pause, doors shut. For thirteen times.

I sighed. My arms ached from holding the stuff from the store, so I stood with my back in the corner of the elevator and slid down until I was sitting on the floor holding the two bags.

Just before the doors closed, a thin bald-headed man with a long fringe of straight black hair ran into the elevator. He was out of breath and sweating a lot, and he kept mopping his head with his handkerchief. He sighed as the elevator stopped at every floor, and finally he turned around to look at me as if I might be responsible. I lifted my shoulders in a resigned shrug to show that I was just as innocent and disgusted as he was.

At the seventh floor the elevator doors opened to reveal Goober.

"Hi, Dad," said Goober, stepping into the elevator. "I just took the books down to Mr. Holloway like I promised."

"Thanks, Goober," said Goober's father.

Goober kept talking. He didn't see me. "He says to tell you he's feeling much better, and thanks for all the reading you've been supplying him with."

Then he looked around and saw me and blinked. He eyed the bunches of bananas that were on top of both bags.

"I see you're laying in a good supply," he said.

I pretended to yawn. "Yes, because I'm hibernating now," I said, shutting my eyes.

"Dad, this is the kid I was telling you about," whispered Goober. "The janitor's son. The one with the banana thing."

I kept my eyes closed, but I knew the father must be turning around to look at me.

Goober kept whispering.

The elevator door opened, paused, shut, opened, paused, shut, two or three more times. We must be on fourteen by now. I opened my eyes. The father had put his arm around Goober, as if they were real pals. I could read his mind.

He was saying to himself, "I may not have the most handsome son in the world, but at least he has all his marbles."

My father could out-pal Goober's father any day of the week. I kept sitting there as they started to get out at fourteen. Goober held the door open. "Do you want me to go up with you to help with the bananas?" he asked.

I shifted my position, and I guess it looked to them as if I was clutching my banana bags.

"Don't worry, we're not going to take them from you," said Goober's father. They exchanged glances, and I read that silent little message, too. It was, "We'll have to play along with him, not alarm him or anything, you know how these loonies are."

The father turned pleasantly to me and said, "I understand your father's the janitor here. Maybe you'll be kind enough to tell him that our kitchen faucet leaks." He paused. "I'm Goober's father, Otto Grube," he said politely.

"How do you do, Mr. Grube," I said. They both waited for me to say my name, and of course I would have automatically as it's a reflex action to be polite in introductions, but the doors closed before I could open my mouth. They still didn't know my last name, thank goodness.

As soon as the elevator got to the next floor (fifteen), I stood up and loped to the stairway with my bags. One of them was going to break open, I knew, and it did, just as I was halfway down the stairs. It was really a mess, and it took forever to get everything into the apartment, racing from the stairway to our door, back and forth, afraid all the time that Goober would come out of their apartment and see me.

"What on earth are you doing?" asked Mom as I made my third trip into the apartment with ice cream and cans of sauce and bunches of bananas.

"It's too hard to explain," I told her. "But it has something to do with that character down the hall. He's giving me a nervous breakdown."

"Aha," nodded Mom.

We unpacked everything, and then I quickly made myself a banana split while Mom was in the shower and went in to watch TV and work on my questionnaire.

WHO DO YOU CONSIDER THE MOST IMPOR-TANT INFLUENCE ON YOUR LIFE, EXCLUDING FAMILY MEMBERS?

Well, except for Dad and Mom, there wasn't anybody in my life. Except Goober, of course.

Although I will not name him for fear of embarrassing this kindly old man, the most important influence in my life is a simple, unassuming neighbor. We share our ideas and our innermost feelings. We question each other, searching for life's answers. I call upon him whenever I am in trouble. He is always there, ready with a new probing question or a new incisive comment.

Without this elderly friend, my life would be entirely different. Something would be lacking.

What would be lacking, of course, would be this nagging sensation that Goober was going to drive me bananas.

The next day just before the party, I realized I'd eaten all the peanuts that I'd bought for the banana splits, so I went out to get some more.

When I got back, I got off the elevator at fifteen, as usual, and walked down to our floor. I peered out—no Goober. I was beginning to get really mad at him and at myself because why should I be sneaking around this way? Just because I didn't want to wind up having Goober for my friend all summer?

I walked to our apartment door and started to turn my key in the lock. It just didn't work. The key turned, but the door was stuck.

I knocked and Mom came to the other side of the door and tried to pull, and I tried to push, and nothing happened. "It's stuck," she called through the door. "I'll call the janitor."

"It just takes a little force," I said, and I started to push harder against the door. "Stand out of the way, Mom," I called. I stepped back a couple of paces and then ran forward, banging against the door hard with my shoulder.

"A couple more tries," I called through the door. I stepped back again, and once more I threw all my weight against the door.

The elevator doors opened, and Goober stepped off the elevator. He saw me just as I was giving it one more try. This time it worked, and I flew headlong into our apartment.

Goober was right on my heels.

"Stop!" he shouted.

Then he saw Mom standing in the middle of the living room, looking surprised, and he yelled, "Give him your bananas! Give him all you've got! Don't argue, don't struggle!"

Turning to me, he said (soothingly), "Now, this nice lady will give you any bananas she has, don't you worry, and then you can come over to our apartment. We've got a whole lot of bananas, honest, we bought a whole batch of them just this morning. We'll see that you get all the bananas you want. Just don't harm this innocent lady."

Mom started to laugh, and Goober turned to her and said, "It's all right, madam, please don't be hysterical. You've had a close call, but everything is going to be all right."

He glared at me. "You've gone too far! Breaking down doors! Threatening innocent women! You really must have some psychiatric attention. I'll ask my father. He has connections. He can help."

Mom sat down on the couch, still laughing.

"Actually, this is my mother," I said coldly. I didn't see anything funny about the situation. Goober was too much.

His pimples started to turn brighter. "It's one thing to threaten a stranger, but your own *mother.* That's despicable."

He turned to Mom. "I suggest that if you have any bananas that you give them to him immediately in order to avoid any further unpleasantness. You may not have realized it until now, but your son has a strange fixation about bananas. Sometimes parents are the last to realize—"

"Thank you for warning me," said Mom. "Jonah, I don't think you've introduced me to your friend," she said to me.

My friend! I glared at Goober. "This is my mother, this is Goober Grube who lives on this floor."

Goober wasn't listening. "Your son may seem to you perfectly normal, although—"

"Oh, on the contrary," said Mom smiling. "Wouldn't you like to stay and have some carrot juice or something?"

"I'd be happy to stay until he quiets down. And if you would like as an added precaution for me to call my father, I can get in touch with him. He already knows something of your son's problems."

Mom smiled at him. "I don't think we need to

worry," she assured him. "He seems quiet now."

Goober looked over at me. "That can be very deceptive," he said as if I wasn't even there. "He is docile and reasonable one minute and raving the next. Bananas seem to trigger some very odd behavior."

"I never dreamed," murmured Mom. "And I have so many here now, he might become violent." Then she started to laugh again. "Goober, I'm having a party. Won't you stay and help Jonah make banana splits?"

"I'd be glad to," said Goober. He glanced over at me and then turned back to Mom.

"I'll just dash over to our apartment for a minute to change," he said. "I'll be right back. You're sure you'll be all right?"

Mom nodded. "If he runs amok again, I'll yell. You'll hear me, I'm a loud screamer."

Before he left, Goober screwed his face up into one of his ugly masks, this one Mr. Holier than Thou.

"A nice polite boy," said Mom.

"A real freak," I said.

"All in the eye of the beholder. He seems to think you're a raving maniac."

"I will be if I hang around with him," I told her.

"Well, he seems like a bright boy," said Mom.

"Glows in the dark," I sighed.

When Goober came back a couple of minutes later I saw that he had changed his shorts and shirt and had plastered his hair down. It didn't improve his appearance.

Then the guests started arriving, and Goober and I went out to the kitchen. My deal with Mom was that I wouldn't have to meet the ladies. Twelve ladies equals one million questions. Goober and I would make the banana splits and signal her when they were ready. Then we'd go out the back way and take ours over to his apartment. I'd help Mom with the dishes later.

Goober and I lined up everything for the banana splits. We figured out who would do what. Ice cream scoops: Goober. Sauces: me. Bananas: Goober. Nuts: me. Marshmallow sauce: Goober. Maraschino cherries: me.

It was like an operating room scene. Intense and quiet. It was time for the bananas. Goober glanced over at me. "Got a bowl?" he whispered.

I nodded and got one out. "We'll want to wash the bananas," he said.

"What for?" I asked. "No one will be eating the skins."

"I thought you always washed your bananas," said Goober.

"You're crazy," I said. "When you wanted water for your guppies that day I thought—"

But it was too hard to explain.

Goober carefully placed each banana in the bowl of water before he peeled it, glancing over at me each time. "Now you're sure you won't mind if I cut into them?" he asked, his eyes bulging. "That's a lot of bananas to kill."

"Tell you what," I whispered. "You cut them. I just won't watch, okay?"

He nodded and set about his task. We had to work quickly so that the ice cream wouldn't get soft.

After we'd dished up all the banana splits, I signaled Mom with a whistle. She came out to the kitchen and gasped at the huge plates of goop, gasped and laughed.

"Mind-swoggling," she whispered. "I'll never hear the end of it!"

Goober and I took ours out the back way to his apartment—kitchen door, back corridor, down, around, up and then his apartment.

We sat on the living room floor with them as usual because as usual there was nowhere else to sit.

"You exaggerated about the size of your family," said Goober, pushing his ice cream around. "There's not room in that apartment for ten children. That would mean twelve people. You lied about the size of your family *and* the location of your apartment," he added accusingly.

He slurped and swallowed, chewed and burped. I didn't say anything. Then he said, "You probably lied because you have something you're hiding. Perhaps your parents are divorced. These days that is not the rarity that it was in days gone by, it's nothing to be ashamed of. You will find as you mature that only the truth serves. In your insecurity you felt you had to fabricate."

"It was only a tale told by an idiot, signifying nothing," I murmured.

"Actually, you got through the preparations for that party very well, considering your attachment to bananas. Your mother is a wise person. Surrounding you with quantities of bananas turned out to be a very sensible experiment. Being exposed to—"

I'd been trying to think of what to put down as my intended career (PROFESSIONAL AMBITIONS) on the Fairlee Questionnaire, and now I started to consider *Psychiatrist.* I could double-talk and fake a lot if I kept listening to Goober.

He chattered on, spilling sauce on his shirt. "You may have some inner guilts or anxieties that you've hidden away from your conscious mind," he was saying. "They plague you without your realizing it. Your problem surfaces with your banana fixation and your evasiveness, and that keeps you from realizing your fullest potential."

By the time we'd finished our banana splits, I had figured out my paragraph: WHY I HAVE CHOSEN PSYCHIATRY AS MY PROFESSION:

I chose psychiatry because I would like to help my patients face up to the inner guilts and anxieties that plague them and that keep them from realizing their fullest potential.

I'd have to look up how to spell anxieties, plague, and potential, but it had a pretty sincere ring.

7 · It Was Hopeless, So I Didn't Try Too Hard

Now that Goober knew where I lived, I didn't stand a chance. He started coming over at odd hours of the day. He talked through my television programs. I kept turning the sound louder and louder but he kept talking louder and louder. I tried to get rid of him, but it was like getting rid of a long summer cold that hangs on and on and on, and just as you think you've sneezed your last sneeze it starts all over again.

Then for days he wouldn't show up. I'd have started to relax when he'd appear at the door with another emergency of his or else just to sit at our apartment and ruin my day.

Between times I'd work on the questionnaire. Actually, I've got to admit that I picked Goober's brains when I was around him, and I used all kinds of stuff he'd say for the questionnaire that helped me a lot. Things like "Give your opinion of the results of the Vietnam War," or "Have you any political preference?"

I'd get him started talking, and then I'd take mental notes and copy them down after he'd left. That way I finished up the questionnaire without too much more monkey business. I'd kept postponing the hard part.

WHAT IS YOUR SELF-IMAGE? DO YOU CONSIDER YOURSELF TOO TALL, TOO SHORT, TOO FAT, TOO LEAN?

DO YOU THINK YOU PRESENT AS GOOD AN IMAGE AS THE NEXT BOY?

I'd been thinking about that one a lot. If I admitted that I was too short and too fat, then maybe they'd never let me keep too much stuff in that refrigerator I was going to have very soon. They might not, anyway, once they got a look at me. Of course I'm not really that fat, it's just that I'm going through this stage.

Finally I wrote:

One's self-image is not just what one sees in a mirror. When I look at myself through others' eyes, I see a young boy who has not yet outgrown his youthful body. There will be changes, there will be improvements. I believe in the old Latin expression, which I will here translate, a sound mind in a sound body.

As far as presenting as good an image as my peers, I can only say that I do not look at my friends' imperfections, but only at the real person that looks out from their eyes. I can only hope that they are looking at the hidden me, and not at the boyish image I present to the world.

After I'd written it, I got up and looked in the mirror. If anybody could see any hidden me, they had better eyes than mine.

Dad was out of town, Mom had gone to dinner and a show with a couple of her friends, and I was settling down in front of the television set, ready for a great night. I'd mailed off the Fairlee Questionnaire, and I felt relaxed. Also, I hadn't seen Goober all day, which had given my stomach and my nerves a chance to settle down.

I'd just turned on my favorite program, my hamburgers were cooking away, and I had a big box of pretzels beside me to tide me over until the hamburgers were ready, when there was this knocking at the door.

It was Goober. He was all bug-eyed, and his pimples were not so pink as blue, and when I opened the door he gasped, "Hurry!" and turned and ran across the hall to his apartment.

Another non-emergency, I thought to myself. But you never knew. Maybe it was something important. Sometime he'd be calling "Wolf, Wolf" when there really was a wolf. Maybe a wolf was attacking his parents right now. That's the way he was acting, anyway. It was either that or some other nameless catastrophe, so I ran after him.

He raced into his apartment and into his room. He pointed wildly to the aquarium.

"It's leaking, it's leaking seriously! We've got

to transfer all of them into the bathtub! We've got to hurry!" He squinted desperately at his watch. "They'll be closing," he whispered. "The pet shop will be closing, and I've got to get another aquarium. The bathtub is just a temporary solution."

He leaned over the aquarium and gasped. "The water's going down fast. We've got to be quick. I've started the water in the tub. You transfer the fish while I run over to the pet shop for the aquarium."

He was already opening and shutting his bureau drawers, looking for his wallet. The reason I knew this is that he kept saying, "Wallet, Wallet, Wallet," as if it would hear him and say, "Here I am."

"Don't look at me," I said. "I'm not carrying those fish into another room, I'm not carrying them anywhere."

"They'll die, they'll die!" said Goober, his eyes bulging.

It reminded me of the first time I'd met him.

"You move them, I'll get the new aquarium," I suggested.

"Look," he said urgently. "All you have to do

is to lift them out with this net, into this bowl, and then you take the bowl into the bathroom and spill them into the tub very gently."

I shook my head.

"They won't bite or anything," he said.

That did it. I didn't want him to think I was afraid of them, even though they were pretty darn slippery. "Well, hurry," I said. "I'm really busy."

People downgrade television, but it's true that if there's something you've really been looking forward to watching and then you have to transfer someone's fish or something instead, it's a big disappointment.

Goober finally found his wallet and dashed out of the apartment. I tried fishing the fish out of the leaking aquarium with the little net. It really was leaking fast, and pretty soon the fish wouldn't have any water at all. I had gotten three in the bowl and was just lifting out the fourth when I suddenly remembered I'd forgotten to turn down the heat under the hamburgers that I was fixing for supper. They were probably burning right now and probably setting our whole kitchen on fire.

In my hurry I dropped the fourth fish, a black one, on the floor, and it was sort of jumping around on the carpet, and I wanted to save it but I had to get to our apartment or the whole thing might catch on fire, maybe the whole building. So I dashed out of Goober's apartment and into ours, and sure enough there was smoke all over the living room, to say nothing of the kitchen, and in another minute it would have been a real disaster, comparable to a wolf attacking Goober's parents in their beds.

I turned off the stove and then dashed back to Goober's to save that fish that I'd left flopping on the floor. I got him into the net and into the bowl, and he looked pretty sickly to me, but maybe he'd revive when I got him into the tub.

The tub. I'd forgotten it. The water was still running, I could hear it now. I raced into the bathroom and sure enough, the tub was overflowing, and there was about an inch in the bathroom and it had spilled out into the hallway.

Before I had a chance to have a real nervous breakdown I heard the door to the apartment open and I yelled, "Goober!" and it wasn't Goober, it was his father.

He stood there looking at me strangely. He'd look at me more strangely still if he saw the mess I'd made with the overflowing tub and all.

"Where's Goober?" he asked.

"He had an errand to do," I said, hoping he wouldn't hear the water running.

If he waited here for Goober I'd be in trouble because I'd made a real mess, so I said, "He asked if you could meet him. It's very important. Meet him at the drugstore over on Diamond and Royal as soon as possible."

Mr. Grube frowned and kept on frowning.

"He said to hurry," I urged him. "He's all right and everything, but he needs to talk to you right away."

Mr. Grube, still frowning, turned to go. Then he turned back.

"What about the faucet?"

"The faucet?" I asked.

"Our kitchen faucet is leaking. Be sure to tell your father."

"Oh, I'm sure he'll be very interested," I said. All I could think of was that overflowing tub.

"Don't forget," he said.

I nodded. "I'll be writing to him tonight, and

I'll mention it," I said. "He'll be very interested to hear about it. He loves faucets."

"Writing to him?" His black eyebrows shot up. Now I remembered that my father was supposed to be the janitor here. It was too hard to explain everything, so I just said, "Well, he's very hard of hearing, so we either shout at him or we write him notes. I don't have a very loud voice, so I usually write to him instead of shouting."

If I didn't get rid of him this minute, the water would start coming into the living room.

"You'd better hurry over to that drugstore," I told him. "It's a really big emergency of some kind."

Mr. Grube looked as if he was as used to Goober's non-emergencies as I was, but he opened the door to leave. "Don't forget about the faucet," he said as he left.

I fled to the bathroom, which meant wading through water. I hurried to make the best of things. I turned off the water in the tub, and I grabbed every towel in sight to soak up the water on the bathroom floor. It was hopeless, so I didn't try too hard. I ran back into Goober's room to see how the fish were doing, the fish in the little bowl and the fish still left in the leaky aquarium. The fish in the little bowl were sickly, and the fish in the aquarium were flopping all around, and I didn't see how I could ever get them out with a net, I'd have to do it by hand, and I decided I would either faint, or be sick, or have a nervous breakdown, or die.

About fifty hours later I had all the fish in the bathtub, and everything was just about as wet as the bathtub was. Goober's room, where the aquarium had leaked, and the bathroom, and the hallway, and me, and probably the floor below that and the floor below that.

And where was Goober, I wondered angrily. It would be a year before my TV program was on rerun, and I'd probably be too old for it by then, at the rate I was aging.

I was beginning to feel really sorry for myself, mushing about with towels trying to get everything dried up, when Goober burst into the apartment, carrying a huge aquarium that was about twice as big as he was. His face loomed through the glass. He looked kind of like a big fish.

"I got it, I got it," he said. "How are they? Did you save them all?"

"I saved them all," I said, suddenly feeling very proud, and suddenly realizing that it was the first time in my life I'd ever felt proud of anything. "They're going to be all right," I went on, reveling in this new sensation. "I think the little black one may be kind of tired, but—"

"You mean Daphne?" he asked, racing into the bathroom. "Maybe she needs—"

Daphne proved to be recovering, and after a lot of arguing about whether I was or was not going to stay and help get the new aquarium ready, I stayed. Actually, I'd have been disappointed if he hadn't needed me. If the *fish* hadn't needed me.

We transplanted the plants, and he put some special capsules in the new water so it would be right for the fish, and then he said we'd have to wait a little while before we put them into the new water. That's when I left.

He said, "Thanks a lot, that was nice of you," the automatic record of anyone who's been brought up well.

Ordeal by fire (the hamburgers) and water (the bathtub overflowing), I thought wearily as I went back to the apartment. I'd have to get things cleaned up before Mom came back.

There was nothing on TV now but the news and the weather reports and the sports reports. Goober had ruined my whole evening, he was ruining my disposition, he was ruining my summer.

8 · This Calls for a Celebration

I was starting to have nightmares about the stupid questionnaire. I'd mailed it in, yes, but had I answered the questions right? Had I sounded sincere enough? Or would they see through all the syrupy goop I'd written to the Real Me—the big fraud?

I checked the mailbox about every hour on the hour, getting a candy bar each time to calm my nerves. What if I didn't get in? *No television.* None at all. The prospect boggled my mind.

You'd think I had enough problems, what with worrying about whether or not I'd get into Fairlee, and trying to keep away from Goober, but I had one other problem: Dad. He got me awake in the morning for push-ups, he dragged me out every afternoon for long dumb walks, he was going to make an athlete of me, presto chango. His theory about all this exercise was that it built you up, but with me it worked the other way around. It was tearing me down. I wasn't used to all that breathing.

This day was typical. "You can't drift any longer, my boy," he said, striding along while I was trying to keep from keeling over. "You've got to zero in on your future career. Now, I don't want to tell you what to do, but I strongly urge you to consider—"

I'd heard this particular lecture about ninety times. It would be a million years before I was old enough to think about a career, for crumb's sake. I needed time to just relax, watch television, decide at my leisure what I wanted to be a million years from now.

We'd already walked about sixty blocks, and he was just getting started. I was thinking maybe I could pretend to twist my ankle and ride back in a taxi.

". . . television," he said. My ears pricked up. I hadn't been listening. "That's the culprit," he went on. "It's the major factor in the decline of academic excellence. It's turned this nation into a nation of passive viewers. As for sports—" Here he sighed, shook his head, and marched doggedly on. "Spectator sports. People don't play football or basketball anymore, they watch someone else playing."

I'd have to try to keep this conversation from turning into a Let's Get Television lecture, but I was out of breath.

"Television has been the most destructive invention of mankind," Dad said. I could see where this monologue was heading. He'd probably get home and toss the television set right out the window.

"You know, Dad," I panted, "I saw a very interesting program the other night. On the educational channel." I practically shouted the word educational so he'd listen. "It was all about," (I thought quickly), "Careers, and How to Choose Them. It made me realize that I have no time to lose. It was a very, very good program. It honestly made me think. And I decided then and there that television was really terrific. I mean, a whole *program* about choosing a career."

"Hmm," said Dad, striding along, his head up, his shoulders back, his hair blowing in the breeze.

I talked faster. "They showed the advantages and the disadvantages of every single career in the world."

"Sounds like a very ambitious program," he said.

"Well, it certainly opened my eyes, Dad. I hadn't really given it much thought before. But that *television* program was very, very *educational.* It really *inspired* me."

The thing was, I couldn't think of one single career to mention in case he asked me.

He was just taking a deep breath to ask me which career I was interested in, so I said, "Tell me about when you were my age, Dad. Tell me how you chose your career."

That got to him. It's his favorite subject. If he didn't start every third conversation with "When I was your age," I never would have guessed that he had ever been my age or any age except the age he is.

Talking about his boyhood and how terrific he'd been kept him going until we got back to the apartment building. I could save the sprained ankle trick for another time.

We got into the elevator. Dad held the door open for someone, and it turned out to be Mr. Grube. Mr. Grube nodded at me. "Good morning," he said. My father cleared his throat, meaning I should introduce them. He's always very anxious for me to be polite.

"This is my father, Mr. Grube," I said. "Dad, this is Mr. Grube, the father of a friend of mine." That was something else my parents had taught me, telling who is who in one small statement when you introduce people.

Mr. Grube and my father shook hands. Mr. Grube leaned towards Dad and shouted, "NICE DAY!" Dad was pretty startled. "ABOUT OUR KITCHEN FAUCET!" shouted Mr. Grube.

"I don't understand," said Dad.

Mr. Grube reached in his pocket and pulled out a little notebook and pencil. He wrote busily and then tore out the sheet and handed it to Dad. I looked over. It said KITCHEN FAUCET LEAKS. URGENT YOU COME. GRUBE, 1410.

Dad read the note. He looked over at Mr. Grube pleasantly. "I'm sure I don't—"

We had arrived at the fourteenth (thirteenth) floor. "NICE TO HAVE MET YOU," shouted Mr. Grube. "TOMORROW AT THE LATEST. YOU'LL WANT TO BRING SOME WASHERS!"

"Strange man," whispered Dad, when Mr. Grube was safely in his apartment. "You say he's the father of your friend?"

I nodded. It was too hard to explain about Goober and Mr. Grube and about how Mr. Grube thought Dad was the janitor and hard of hearing and all that.

"Strange," Dad repeated, as we walked along the corridor to our apartment.

"There are a lot of oddballs living here," I told him.

When we walked into the apartment, Mom ran in from the kitchen, waving an envelope in the air. "You're in, you made it, you're a Fairlee Boy now!" she said, running over to hug me.

I was in!

Dad clapped me on the shoulder, one of those man-to-man claps that rattle my teeth. "Good boy, good boy," he said, making me feel like a dog that's learned how to retrieve a stick.

I'd made it! All of a sudden I liked my parents better, I liked Goober better, I liked myself better.

"This calls for a celebration," said Mom. I thought for one second that she was going to bring out a cake or something, at least a candy bar, but no. She found some diet ginger ale and poured it into three champagne glasses. My parents don't drink any alcohol, they're very conservative that way, but they put even orange juice into fancy cocktail glasses.

We toasted each other, they toasted me. We all started to talk at once. Dad said he'd take us out for dinner that night. Seeing them so excited made me feel good. I'd done something for the first time in my life that made them happy. I wasn't so bad after all, they weren't so bad after all.

After a while I started to read the letter from Fairlee. It was all about how pleased they were to be able to look forward to the delightful prospect of such a good group, such an *unusually* good group, of new Fairlee Boys.

What had done it? My professional ambitions? My hobbies? My autobiography? What I look for in a friend? My self-image? All those lies?

It didn't matter now. I was in.

There were still several pages to read. Mom said, "By the way, Jonah, Goober came over an hour ago. He wants to see you. He said it was important."

I groaned. Then I lifted my glass in a toast. "Getting away from Goober will be super," only I pronounced it soober. "I'll see him later," I promised. "His emergencies are too traumatic for me today."

I started to read the rest of the letter. They had weighed the answers in the questionnaires and had selected for every Fairlee Boy a roommate who would be congenial. For me, Jonah, they had selected a boy who would share my interests and ideals and aspirations, who would be a lifelong friend to the boy I am today and to the man I will be tomorrow. His name was Lewis K. Trane, Jr.

They suggested the appropriate kind of clothing I should get: everything navy blue and red and white—I was going to look like an American flag, but I didn't care.

I hadn't even finished reading the letter when

there was a knock at the door. It was Goober, wheezing and coughing and pimpling. "Hurry!" he said. "We've got to get the baby guppies out of the aquarium. They're being eaten. Hurry."

I sighed and turned to follow him. Then I turned back and winked at Mom and Dad. "See what a good sport I am?" I asked. "A real Fairlee Boy, already."

9 · Only The Beginning

It took a couple hundred hours to get the baby fish safely in another aquarium. By now Goober had three new aquariums. And he'd bought some new fish—swordtails and black mollies and neon tetras. And snails and a hideous catfish and some more green stuff and more pills to put in the water to purify and sanctify it.

I couldn't escape Goober any more than his fish could escape from the aquariums. But now it didn't matter. Summer would be over, and I'd be going to Fairlee, and I'd be rooming with a guy named Lewis K. Trane, Jr., and I'd have my own television set and my own refrigerator.

In the next couple of weeks Fairlee sent me a

ton of stuff. They must have a gigantic public relations staff or something. There were all kinds of letters and directives and suggestions and a whole lot of compliments about what a great school Fairlee was and what a great guy I was for getting in. I'd never felt so IN in my life.

They had one of those computer typewriters so that it looked as if every single letter was directed only to me, Jonah, and all through the letter they'd mention my name, but you could tell it was all done automatically, and Lewis K. Trane and all those other guys would be getting the same letter, only theirs would keep saying, "We'll be glad to have you aboard, Lewis, or Gustav, or Gerald or Gary," while mine said, "We'll be glad to have you aboard, Jonah."

I was beginning to feel pretty popular with all the mail I was getting, even if it was just form letters.

I did get one fairly personal letter from them telling how well matched Lewis K. Trane and Jonah D. Krock were as roommates, and what great guys we both were, and how we shared so many interests and hobbies and so on. I was pretty sure that Lewis K. Trane, Jr. had souped up and syruped up the questionnaire as much as I had.

It was a Saturday, and Goober had been bugging me all morning about coming over to help him clean up his aquariums. I finally gave in just to get him off my back.

After we cleaned the aquariums we sat on the living room floor to have our banana splits. I looked again at the boxes on the living room chairs and couches, trying to figure out whether they were the same boxes or different ones each time. Different. Now there was a big one that looked as if it might have a coat or something in it, and that bunch of little boxes that had been on the green chair a couple of days ago wasn't there anymore, just a hat box or something that looked as if there could be a hat inside.

Goober's mother must shop a lot. She never was home, so I guessed that she spent her time shopping, buying things, bringing them home, and going out and buying more things the next day. Or—maybe exchanging them all the next day. That would keep her busy. Some people had pretty boring lives.

Goober was talking away as usual and getting

marshmallow sauce on his cheeks.

". . . to be when you grow up?"

"I am grown up," I said. "I just look very, very young for my age. Actually, I'm thirty-two."

He didn't listen. "I've decided to be a psychiatrist," he said, chomping on a banana.

"I thought you were one already," I said.

He started to mash up his banana split. "It's wise to select your profession when you're young," he said. "That way you can center your interests."

"I thought your interests were fish of various shapes and sizes," I said.

"Tropical fish are my *hobby,*" he corrected me. "You have to have hobbies for purposes of relaxation. It's best to try a variety of hobbies while you're young. Then when you grow up and are a business or professional man you can relax with your hobbies from the pressures of your days."

He was mopping up the rest of his banana split. I'd finished my last bite, so I stretched and stood up. There was a rattling at the door. It was Goober's mother, Mrs. Grube.

"Darling boy, do help me with these packages," she called. Goober and I both went to the door. "Oh, and it's your nice friend. Have you come about the faucet?" she asked.

I shook my head and reached for a couple of the boxes she was balancing in her arms.

"An absolutely madly exhausting day," moaned Mrs. Grube. "Dreadful, wild, devastating day." She started for a chair but it was covered with other boxes. She pushed them off and sank into it gratefully. "It's too much, too much," she murmured. "Ghastly people, I don't know what the city is coming to."

Goober carried our bowls out to the kitchen. Mrs. Grube rummaged in her purse.

"I picked up the mail, darling boy." She looked vaguely in my direction. "Be a love and put it on the dining room table." She flourished a handful of envelopes in the air. I took them and put them on the dining room table. The top one caught my eye. It was from Fairlee School. I'd know their stationery anywhere. And it was addressed to Lewis K. Trane, Jr.

I stood there staring at it stupidly, wondering how it got here.

Goober wandered back from the kitchen.

"A letter from that school for you, precious boy," called Mrs. Grube. "Forwarded finally. When *will* they get our new address?"

I stared at Goober. He was picking his nose.

"What is your name?" I asked slowly and distinctly.

He blinked his bulging eyes.

"What do you mean, what's my name?"

"I thought it was Goober Grube."

"Oh, that. Goober's my nickname, of course. And Grube is my stepfather's name. When Mom married him I just kept my same old name, Trane. Funny you never knew that. You never asked me, and I never thought to tell you."

"So you're Lewis K. Trane," I said stupidly.

"Junior," he amended. "The K is for Knowlton. It's a family name. How come you're so interested in names all of a sudden?"

Mrs. Grube called in from the living room. "I'm going to take a bubble bath, darling boy."

Goober hadn't read his letter from Fairlee so he didn't know yet that I was to be his new roommate or even that I was going to Fairlee, too.

He glanced down at the table. "Oh, I see why

you wondered about my name. This letter. Well, it's from some school I was trying to get into." He opened it and glanced at it. "Okay. I got in. I knew I would." He looked at me with his bulgy eyes. "Since I'll be away at school this year, would you take care of my fish for me?" He blinked and added, "Or maybe they'll let me bring the fish. It's worth a try."

So much for starting fresh. Just as I'd thought I could write Amen, Finis, The End to my friendship with Goober, I could see it was Only the Beginning.

Fairlee, here I come.

ABOUT THE AUTHOR

FLORENCE PARRY HEIDE is the author of many books, including *The Shrinking of Treehorn* (an A.L.A. Notable Book), *When the Sad One Comes to Stay, Growing Anyway Up,* and a series of juvenile mysteries which she writes with her daughter Roxanne. A native of Pittsburgh, Pennsylvania, and a graduate of the University of California, Mrs. Heide lives in Kenosha, Wisconsin. She is married to an attorney, Donald Heide, and they have three sons and two daughters.